# NANCY CLANCY

## Star of Stage and Screen

WRITTEN BY
**Jane O'Connor**

ILLUSTRATIONS BY
**Robin Preiss Glasser**

**HARPER**
*An Imprint of HarperCollinsPublishers*

ISBN 978-0-06-226963-8

Typography by Jeanne L. Hogle

16 17 18 19  CG/OPM  10 9 8 7 6 5 4 3 2
❖
First paperback edition, 2016

For JoJo—I mean Jilly (aka Jill Abramson)

—J.O'C.


For Yarden, our star

—R.P.G.

# CONTENTS

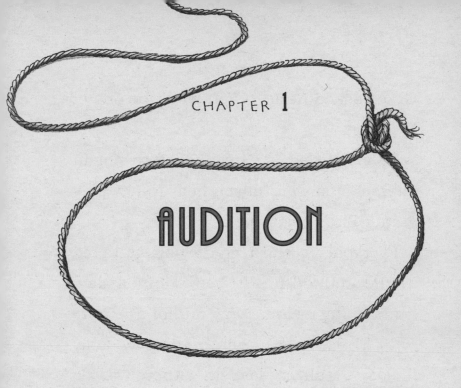

# CHAPTER 1

# AUDITION

Nancy kept licking her lips. The inside of her mouth felt as dry as dust. Her tummy was doing flip-flops and she was perspiring like crazy. Perspiring sounded more grown-up—and less gross—than sweating.

"What are you so worked up about?"

Grace asked Nancy. "You won't be one of the stars."

Bree scowled at Grace. "You're not in charge. Just wait till you hear Nancy play guitar. She's awesome."

Everyone in third grade had gathered in the auditorium. It was audition day. Auditioning meant trying out for *The Nifty Fifty*. That was the name of the play. Only it wasn't really a play, since there was no story. It was more like a variety show with lots of nifty—Mr. D explained that meant cool—songs and dances all about the fifty states.

Yesterday Mr. Dudeny had told the class, "Our third-grade performance is one of the highlights of the school year. So come prepared to show off your special talent."

Today Nancy had brought in her guitar. For months she'd been taking lessons from a teenager named Andy. She didn't stink, but she wasn't awesome, either. Bree only thought so because she was Nancy's best friend.

One by one, kids got up onstage to perform.

Robert brought a lasso with him. He had been born in Texas. His dream was to be a rodeo star one day. "Yippee-ki-yi-yay!" Robert yelled, while the lasso twirled over his head in a circle.

3

Grace had chosen a song about California.

"California, here I come! Right back where I started from!" Grace sang.

Nancy hated to admit it, but Grace's performance was flawless—she didn't make one mistake! At the end, Grace spread out her arms and smiled with all her teeth showing.

Lionel wore a top hat and black cape. "Please hold the applause till the end," he told everyone. First he did a card trick. Then he told a joke. "What is the smartest state?" Lionel paused before giving the answer. "Alabama. Because it has four As and only one B."

Lionel started to walk offstage. "Oh! I

can also burp to the tune of 'Jingle Bells.' Want to hear?"

"A superb talent, dude. But that won't be necessary." Mr. Dudeny was sitting in the audience with the other third-grade teacher.

When it was Bree's turn, she let out a little squeak. Nancy squeezed Bree's hand for luck. Onstage, Bree did a tap dance to a song about New York City. She had on real black patent-leather tap shoes. The little metal pieces on the bottoms made every step ring out in the auditorium. *Clickety-clack-clack.*

"East Side, West Side, all around the town," the song began.

*Shuffle, shuffle, step. Spin. Shuffle, shuffle, step. Spin.*

Bree got off to a good start. Then all of a sudden it got harder for her to keep up with the music. At one point, she had to stop and wait to pick up the beat again.

When Bree came back, she slumped down in her seat and pooched out her lips. "I really messed up," she said, still out of breath.

There was no time to console Bree, because Mr. Dudeny was calling out Nancy's name. She stood and forced her feet to walk up the steps to the stage. She remembered her mom's advice: *Don't look at the crowd. Pretend you are in your room playing just for fun.*

Nancy slung the guitar strap over her shoulder.

"A one, and a two, and a three," Nancy began, and then she broke into the opening chords of "Wild Thing." It was an old rock song, the first one Andy had taught

her. Nancy had played it a zillion times. Maybe more.

"Wild thing. You make my heart sing. You make everything groovy!" Nancy sang. By the second chorus, she felt a little more relaxed. Her lips no longer felt stuck to her gums. When she got to the word "groovy" again, Nancy stretched it out and made her voice go low and raspy, the way Andy did. *"Groooooovy!"*

"See! What did I tell you? She was awesome," Bree was saying to Grace as Nancy got back to her seat.

Grace crossed her arms. "The song had *nothing* to do with any of the states."

"It didn't have to," Bree said. "Nancy just had to show her special talent."

Grace frowned but didn't say anything.

Wow! From Grace, saying nothing was
practically like getting a compliment!

CHAPTER **2**

# COWGIRL SAL

"Daddy, please take off that hat!" Nancy said. "You look absurd!" That was a polite way of saying her father looked silly.

He glanced up from his newspaper. "Well, howdy, partner. Didn't hear you come in." A cowboy hat of JoJo's was perched on his head. "You hungry? I can rustle up a snack."

"Sure." Nancy set down her guitar and backpack. "I tried out for *The Nifty Fifty* today."

"Shh! I can't hear!" JoJo was sitting cross-legged on the floor, watching TV. She was wearing a cowboy hat too. Her favorite show, *Cowgirl Sal*, was on.

"I'm Cowgirl Sal. I'm your best pal," JoJo sang along with the theme song. "And I'm comin' to the rescue."

Cowgirl Sal was played by a grown-up actress who had braids and big, fake freckles on her cheeks. Today she was helping a kitten that was stuck in a tree. Nancy's parents thought Cowgirl Sal was a good role model. That meant they wanted JoJo to act just like her.

"I like being a good helper!" Cowgirl Sal said. Then she pointed to the badge on her shirt. It looked like a sheriff's badge, only it said *Good Helper*. JoJo was wearing one just like it.

Nancy followed her father into the kitchen. "I find out tonight if I get a callback. A callback means—" Nancy stopped talking. "Daddy, I can't have a serious discussion with you in that hat. *Pleeeeease* take it off."

"I reckon I can."

While her dad made a PB&J sandwich, Nancy explained, "A callback means you're getting a part."

"Of course you'll get a part. You always do."

"No, Daddy. I mean a real one." In every play, Nancy always got stuck in the chorus. For the second-grade production of *Peter Pan*, she was Pirate Number Seven. In first grade, for *Jack and the Beanstalk*, she had been a villager. This year, she wanted to stand out. Not that she expected to be one of the stars. But getting to be in the spotlight for a moment or two—well, that would be thrilling.

Nancy checked that the receiver on the house phone wasn't off the hook. She had her dad make sure that his cell phone was turned on. Then she took the sandwich up to her room to do her homework.

Name _Nancy Clancy_
Your state _Wisconsin_
Fun fact _____

Madison

Mr. Dudeny had assigned every kid in 3D a different state to study. Nancy's was Wisconsin. For tomorrow she had to find a fun fact about Wisconsin. She also had to draw a map of the state. Using her atlas, Nancy made an outline of Wisconsin in purple Magic Marker and put a gold sticker of a star where Madison—the capital—went.

Suddenly a bell rang. It was the bell on the Top-Secret Special Delivery mail basket.

Nancy jumped up from her desk and reeled in the basket. It hung from a rope between her bedroom window and Bree's.

Bree's note was short. It was written in their new secret code. It took a minute to decipher.

Bree, looking surprised and happy, was right at the window. So Nancy didn't need to write back. When she shook her head no, Bree held up both hands to show that her fingers were crossed.

9  7-15-20  1
3-1-12-12
2-1-3-11 !!!

After that, it was impossible to do more homework. Nancy lay on her bed, staring at a crack in the ceiling. Frenchy came in and snuggled beside her. Twice Nancy went out into the hall and

NEW SECRET CODE (For your eyes only!)

| A = 1 | G = 7 | M = 13 | S = 19 | Y = 25 |
|-------|-------|--------|--------|--------|
| B = 2 | H = 8 | N = 14 | T = 20 | Z = 26 |
| C = 3 | I = 9 | O = 15 | U = 21 | |
| D = 4 | J = 10 | P = 16 | V = 22 | |
| E = 5 | K = 11 | Q = 17 | W = 23 | |
| F = 6 | L = 12 | R = 18 | X = 24 | |

called down to her dad, "Make sure to listen for the phone!"

Finally, right before dinner, there was a call. But it was from Grace. She'd gotten a callback too.

"So did you hear?" Grace asked.

"No. Not yet."

"Aw, too bad," Grace said. "But there have to be some kids in the chorus, right?" Grace was trying to sound sad for Nancy. Still, Nancy couldn't help but wonder if deep down Grace wasn't secretly kind of glad.

# CHAPTER 3

# YOUTUBE SENSATION

"This grub looks mighty tasty!" Nancy's dad said as he set down a big bowl of spaghetti and meatballs on the kitchen table.

"Doug, please. No more cowboy talk." Nancy's mom was scrubbing JoJo's face at the sink. JoJo had put big black Magic Marker freckles on both her cheeks.

19

"Stop!" JoJo cried. "I look like Cowgirl Sal!"

"JoJo, you use Magic Markers on paper. Nothing else." Nancy's mom sounded tired.

"Nancy puts black dots on her ears," JoJo said, squirming.

That was true. Nancy sometimes did it so her ears looked pierced.

"That's—that's different," Nancy's mom sputtered.

Nancy finished setting the table. A cloth napkin was at each place. They were folded to look like flowers.

"Very elegant!" Nancy's mom sat down and put her napkin in her lap. "How did you learn to do this, honey?"

"On YouTube," Nancy told her. "I can make napkins that look like boats too."

"YouTube! There was something in the paper today," her dad said as he served spaghetti to everyone. "A video of a nine-year-old girl singing 'We Shall Overcome' went viral." Her father explained that going viral meant that a video was seen by millions of people. "The girl's mother put it up on YouTube right before Martin

Luther King Day. The kid has been on two morning talk shows! National TV!"

Nancy twirled spaghetti—or pasta, as she preferred to call it—on her fork. "Were either of you ever stars?" she asked her parents. "Not famous stars, like in Hollywood. But stars in a class play?"

"Don't look at me," her mom said. "I

was always in the chorus." Her mom shrugged. "Your father is the performer in the family."

"Really, Daddy? What did you star in?"

"I was in a mime troupe in college. You know that."

Mimes acted stuff out silently. When she was little, Nancy liked to watch her dad pretend to climb a rope or act like he was stuck inside a box.

"But were you ever in a play where you sang or danced or had lots of lines?" Nancy wanted to know.

"Nope. I was only good when I kept my mouth shut."

Nancy's mom laughed. Then she leaned over and kissed Nancy's dad.

At that moment the phone rang. There

was a rule in the Clancy family: no phone calls during dinner.

Nancy jumped out of her chair before either of her parents had a chance to stop her.

It was Mr. Dudeny. He asked Nancy to

bring in her guitar again tomorrow.

Ooh la la!

Double ooh la la!

Triple ooh la la!

She had gotten a callback!

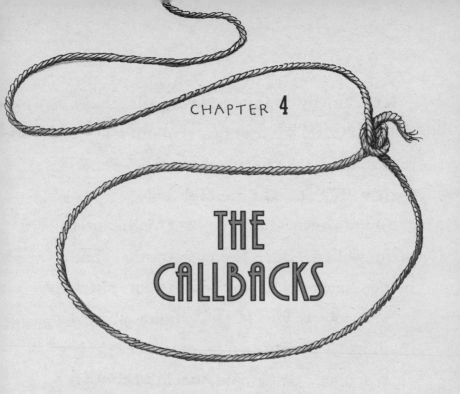

# CHAPTER 4

# THE CALLBACKS

"I got assigned New York," Olivia told the class in social studies. Social studies was the last class of the day. Right after were the callbacks. Olivia read aloud from her homework sheet. "There are more roadside diners in New York than any other state."

Mr. Dudeny thanked Olivia, then said, "Okay, dudes! We just heard about a state on the East Coast. Let's hear from somebody with a state in the Midwest."

Nancy's arm shot up. Last night after JoJo was in bed, Nancy's mother had helped her find out stuff on the computer.

"My state is Wisconsin," Nancy started reading. "It produces a lot of paper."

"Whoopee," Grace said, just loud enough so Mr. Dudeny wouldn't hear and Nancy would.

Nancy ignored Grace and continued, "The city of Green Bay is known as the Toilet Paper Capital of the World. It produces more than a hundred million rolls of toilet paper every year. In the 1930s the first splinter-free toilet paper was invented there."

"You mean people used to get splinters from toilet paper?" Bree wanted to know.

"Ouch!" said Lionel. "That had to hurt!"

Mr. Dudeny was looking around the room. "So who has a state that shares a border with Wisconsin? That means the two states touch. Look on the wall map to see."

Clara raised her hand, then yanked it down. But Mr. Dudeny had spotted her.

"Yes, Clara."

"Iowa?" Clara didn't sound sure.

"Right you are!"

Clara smiled. "It turns out Iowa is the

only state that starts with two vowels."

"Superb fact. I never realized that." Then Mr. Dudeny glanced at his wristwatch. "I am afraid we have to wrap it up for today," he said as the bell rang.

Ooh la la! It was time for the callbacks!

The callback kids met onstage in the auditorium. Bree whispered to Nancy, "I'm nervous. I think it's a mistake to do a tap dance."

"Why? That's your special talent," Nancy said.

"Not really. I'm just a beginner," Bree said. "I'm not that good."

"Hey, why are you here?" Grace was pointing at Nancy. "You didn't get a callback!"

"Oh yes, I did. Mr. D called right after dinner." Nancy was happy to set Grace straight.

A few minutes later, Nancy learned that she was going to be in a duet with Robert. The two of them were going to perform together. Their song was called "Deep in the Heart of Texas."

"I printed out the lyrics," Mr. Dudeny said. Robert, however, didn't need them. He said, "Every kid from Texas knows the words." The way Robert pronounced "Texas," it rhymed with "sixes."

"The song has a simple strum pattern," Mr. Dudeny told Nancy. Then he borrowed her guitar and showed her.

"The stars at night are big and bright— deep in the heart of Texas," he began singing.

Mr. Dudeny was playing only two different chords. They were the first ones Andy had taught Nancy. This was going

to be easy-peasy.

"Nancy, you'll start off onstage alone and sing the first line." Mr. Dudeny turned to Robert. "That's when you enter, Robert. You'll be twirling your lasso and join in for the chorus line, 'Deep in the heart of Texas.'"

Ooh la la! It suddenly hit Nancy. For

a few seconds she'd be onstage all by herself in the spotlight! Not that there was actually a spotlight. But still. The entire audience would be watching her. It was thrilling to imagine—and scary.

Mr. Dudeny handed back Nancy's guitar and left them to start practicing.

First Robert sang the whole song through so the tune stuck in Nancy's head. Then they sang it together. Robert was a quiet boy. However, every time he came to the "Deep in the heart of Texas" line, he yelled it out. He sounded like a genuine cowboy!

"Mr. Dudeny wants me to stick with tap dancing," Bree told Nancy as they walked down the front steps of Ada M. Draezel

Elementary School. "He says all I need is practice." She didn't sound convinced.

"You'll be great. There's almost two weeks till the show."

"Two weeks! That's no time!" Bree swallowed hard. "There are basic steps I don't know yet."

Grace was right behind Nancy and Bree and overheard them. "I sing a song about Oklahoma. What part did you get, Nancy?"

"Robert and I are singing 'Deep in the Heart of Texas.'"

"Oh, so you sing together. Not alone." Grace followed them to the bike rack. "There'll be kids square-dancing in back of me. At the end they spell out Oklahoma. O-K-L-A—"

Nancy and Bree stood there while Grace

finished spelling "Oklahoma."

*Grace is such a show-off!* Nancy didn't say the words out loud. She just thought them. And she could tell Bree heard her. That was one of the many great things about being best friends. A lot of times they didn't even need to speak. They could simply read each other's minds.

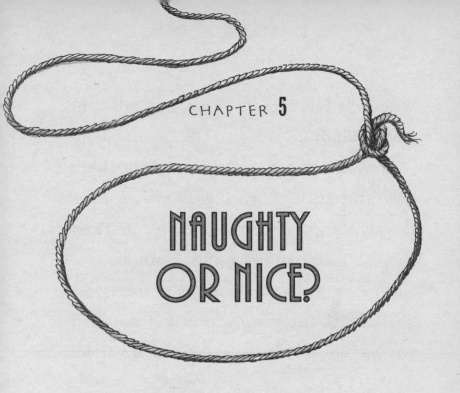

CHAPTER 5

# NAUGHTY OR NICE?

At exactly four thirty, the doorbell started ringing. It was time for Nancy's guitar lesson.

Nancy flung open the door.

"Andy! Guess what! I'm playing guitar in the third-grade variety show!"

"Aw-right!" Andy high-fived Nancy.

When she told him the song, he said, "Oh, you'll nail that."

Andy unlatched his guitar case. There were stickers of old rock groups—the Beatles, Queen, the Doors—all over it. Then they both started tuning their guitars.

Nancy's guitar was her most prized possession. It was turquoise and had imitation ivory knobs on the neck. After giving them

a few twists, Nancy began strumming with her pick. It was imitation ivory too.

"Sounding sweet!" Andy told her. Then he played "Deep in the Heart of Texas" a few times, demonstrating when to switch from D major to A major and back again. "Now, your turn," he said.

"The stars at night," Nancy sang, "are big and bright—deep in the heart of Texas." It was harder singing and strumming simultaneously. That meant doing both at the same time. Nevertheless, by the time JoJo came galloping into the living room on a mop, Nancy was getting the hang of it.

"Whoa!" JoJo told the mop. Then she scooted next to Nancy on the sofa. "Play that song more. I like it."

So Nancy did.

Soon JoJo knew some of the words. It was fun having her sing along. Near the end of the lesson, Andy suggested that Nancy and JoJo try clapping four times before every chorus.

"And ask the audience to clap along with you. Remember, it's not just about playing a song. You want to give the crowd a performance."

Nancy guessed Andy must know what he was talking about. After all, he was becoming a local celebrity. He played at kids' birthday parties as well as bar mitzvahs and sweet sixteens. He was probably on YouTube.

Before dinner Nancy did some homework. For tomorrow she had to add information to her map of Wisconsin. First Nancy made a dot for the city of Green Bay. She was drawing a roll of toilet paper by it when she heard her mother cry, "JoJo! Did Nancy tell you it was okay to do this?"

Nancy whipped downstairs.

*Sacre bleu!* That was French for "Yipes!"

Her guitar case was on JoJo's lap. There were stickers all over it, stickers of Cowgirl Sal; her sidekick, Cowboy Roy; and her pony, Pixie.

Nancy let out a scream and snatched the guitar case. "How could you do this?"

JoJo looked surprised. "I made it look good—like Andy's."

"Are you joking?" Nancy shouted. "It doesn't look like Andy's. It looks absurd."

All at once JoJo's face crumpled and she started crying.

"Nancy, calm down. The stickers will come off." Her mom bent down and said sternly, "JoJo, I have told you many times about respecting other people's property. You—"

"That's right!" Nancy broke in. "Keep

your hands off my stuff. Especially my guitar. It's my most prized possession!"

"Why are you mad?" JoJo said, tears splashing down her cheeks. "It's nice to do special things for your posse."

Argh! JoJo was repeating what Cowgirl Sal said at the end of every show.

"It wasn't nice, and I'm not in your posse."
Then Nancy stormed up to her room.

A few minutes later there was a rap at the door.

"Did the stickers come off?" her mom asked.

Nancy nodded.

"I honestly think JoJo meant to be nice."

Nancy frowned. "Maybe." Then she asked,

"When I was little, was I as naughty as JoJo?"

Nancy's mom blew her bangs off her forehead and thought for a moment. "No, you weren't. Sometimes JoJo can't seem to help herself. . . . She was just born rambunctious." Nancy's mom explained that meant full of mischief but in a fun way.

Nancy didn't answer. Ordinarily, she loved long and complicated words. But in this case, she couldn't see how being rambunctious was really any different from being just plain naughty.

# CHAPTER 6

# PRACTICE MAKES PERFECT

On Wednesday Bree took an extra class at Tappy Feet after school. Robert came home with Nancy to rehearse. He brought his lasso and a silver stopwatch with him. "I can tell to a tenth of a second how long it takes us to sing our song."

"Why? Did Mr. Dudeny say there was a time limit?" Nancy asked.

"No. I got it for my birthday. I like to time stuff." Robert showed her how the stopwatch worked. Then he showed her what else was in his backpack. Lots of Western stuff for Nancy to borrow! There was a brown suede vest with fringe, a blue-and-white-checked handkerchief for Nancy to tie around her neck, and a red cowboy hat.

"*Merci beaucoup*, Robert!" Nancy tried everything on. With her jean skirt and pink cowboy boots, her costume was now complete. Nancy tilted the hat a little and stared at herself in the hall mirror. She could almost hear the applause at the end of their number. Performing in *The Nifty Fifty* was going to be thrilling—the most thrilling moment of her life.

In the kitchen, Nancy offered Robert some refreshments, a plate of cookies and Fruit Roll-Ups. While they were splitting the last cookie, they heard howling outside. It was Frenchy.

Robert followed Nancy out the back door.

Frenchy was in the yard, tied by her leash to a tree. "Ah-woo, ah-woo!" she cried.

Nancy ran to Frenchy, who pawed at her and licked her madly.

"Poor girl! Hold still while I untie you!"

"No! Don't!"

All at once, from around the side of house, JoJo came riding up on her mop. "I'm Cowgirl Sal. I'm your best pal. And I'm comin' to the rescue!" she shouted.

Nancy set Frenchy free, who bounded off into Mrs. DeVine's yard next door.

JoJo dropped her mop. "Why'd you do that?"

Nancy's hands were on her hips. "JoJo, did you tie Frenchy up? You know she hates that!"

"It was only for a minute. I was coming to rescue her!"

"But if you tied her up, then it doesn't count as a rescue. It was mean what you did. Don't you understand that?" Nancy realized she was shouting in front of company. *"Excusez-moi,"* she said to Robert. That meant "Excuse me" in French.

Nancy crossed her arms as her sister rode off. The Cowgirl Sal show was supposed to teach little kids to be kind and helpful. But with JoJo, it was doing the opposite. It was making her naughtier. Nancy wondered why her parents let JoJo keep watching it.

# CHAPTER 7

# MASTER OF CEREMONIES

At lunch the next day, Lionel went from table to table asking for jokes about the states. He was *The Nifty Fifty* master of ceremonies. Emcee for short. He was going to introduce each act.

"I know one," Grace said. "Where do pencils come from?" She waited a second, then said, "Pennsylvania!"

"Not bad," said Lionel, and he wrote it down in a notepad.

Clara also had a joke. "Why do people from Maine act so nutty? . . . Because they're luna—!" Then Clara smacked her forehead. "Oh wait! I goofed. Let me start over. . . . Why do people from Maine act so nutty?" Clara asked again. "Because they're maniacs."

"And here's one for my state," said Bree. "Where do pianists go for vacation—the Florida Keys!"

Lionel wrote both jokes down.

It turned out that Bree had already finished her state page on Florida. She showed it to Nancy that afternoon after school.

"*Sacre bleu!* I've hardly started!" Nancy exclaimed. "We don't have to hand them in till next week."

"I know. But I need tons of time—every spare minute—to rehearse."

Bree was tying the bows on her tap shoes. Nancy had brought over a pair of old clogs with quarters glued to the soles. So now her shoes clickety-clacked too. Sort of.

They went outside to the wooden deck at the back of Bree's house.

"I learned a new step yesterday at Tappy Feet. The brush-and-shuffle. I'm adding it to my dance," Bree said. "Here's how you do it."

Nancy tried copying what Bree did. It was hard! Bree's tap dancing had really improved. In fact, she was looking pretty professional. Yet whenever she made even the teensiest mistake, Bree insisted on starting from the beginning.

"East Side, West Side, all around the town . . . ," Bree sang over and over. It got monotonous—that meant boring. At one point the quarter on Nancy's left clog came off. So Nancy stopped dancing and watched Bree.

"You're good!" Nancy told her. "Your feet got much faster!"

This time Bree made it all the way through to the end. She collapsed in a deck chair, huffing and puffing. "I want to be better than good! I want to be perfect. All I need is practice. Lots of practice."

An hour later, while Nancy helped get dinner ready, she could still hear the New York song playing from Bree's deck.

"East Side, West Side, all around the town."

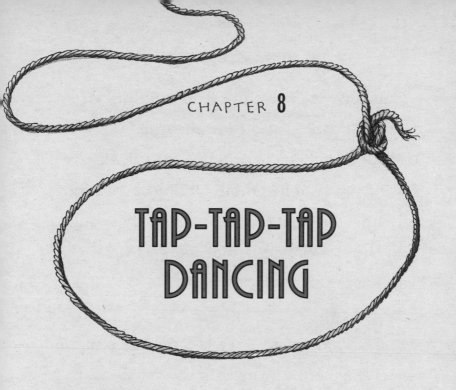

# CHAPTER 8

# TAP-TAP-TAP DANCING

On Friday afternoon Bree skipped soccer practice. On Saturday she missed tea at Mrs. DeVine's house. On Sunday Bree wouldn't go to the movies with Nancy.

"Oh, come on, Bree! The newspaper said it's really funny. It's about a princess who runs away so she can be an ordinary girl."

"No, I can't. I need to rehearse."

"All Bree does is practice for the show," Nancy said to her mom while they waited in line for popcorn. "By now she could do the tap dance in her sleep. But she's so scared of making even one tiny little mistake."

"That's because Bree is a perfectionist," Nancy's mom said as they took their seats.

"Is that good or bad?" Nancy couldn't tell from the way her mother had said it.

"Well, it's good because Bree always wants to do the best she can. She tries super-hard at everything. But making a mistake isn't the worst thing in the world. Everybody makes mistakes."

Then they stopped talking. The coming

attractions were starting.

The next day JoJo stayed home from preschool because she had a cold. Lots of kids in Nancy's class were absent too.

"Tamar, Joel, Nola, Olivia, and Lionel," Nancy told her parents that evening, ticking their names off on her fingers. "Lionel is the master of ceremonies. He has to be back by Friday for *The Nifty Fifty*!"

Dinnertime was very quiet without JoJo at the table.

Later, Nancy's dad brought some soup upstairs for her on a tray. Nancy stood with her guitar by the door to her sister's room. "Want me to play the Texas song for you?" she asked.

JoJo coughed and nodded. She looked so little and sad in her bed. Not rambunctious

at all. It made Nancy want to hug her sister, except JoJo was too germy.

At school on Tuesday, there was a
run-through of the show. Lionel was still
absent so Mr. D took his place as emcee.
It was the first time Nancy got to see many
of the other songs and dances.

For the grand finale—the very last

act—the whole third grade got up onstage. They marched around with signs that said either *Hooray for the USA!* or *The Nifty Fifty* and sang "This Land Is Your Land." Nancy loved the song. It was about how everybody in America was part of one big family, "from California to the New York island."

After the run-through, Bree kept on her tap shoes. At lunch, she tap-danced down the cafeteria line. *Clickety-clack-clack.* She tap-danced to their table under the poster of the five food groups. And when she was finished eating, she tap-danced over to the garbage bins to throw her sandwich bag away. The clicking sound was starting to drive Nancy nuts! Nancy ate fast and ran outside for recess.

"I'll be right out," Bree called to her. "I just need to use the lavatory." And away she tapped.

"Want to jump rope with us?" Tamar asked Nancy in the yard. She had already rounded up a bunch of girls.

"Sure," Nancy said. "I'll be one of the turners."

Then Tamar asked, "Where's Bree?" Except for Grace, Bree was best at double Dutch.

"Oh, Bree's tap-dancing over to the girls' room." Nancy rolled her eyes. "Tap, tap, tap. All she does is tap dance! I'm sick of it. She's—she's too much of a perfectionist!"

A funny expression came over Tamar's face. Her eyes were looking past Nancy.

Nancy spun around. There was Bree. Her lips started to tremble. She blinked a couple of times.

"Well, excuse me for wanting to do a good job!" she finally said.

Then Bree turned and stormed off into the school building.

"It's—it's true what I said!" Nancy stammered to all the girls. But she wished the words could fly back in her mouth. She felt horrible. Nobody said anything. They looked embarrassed.

In the hallway, Nancy caught up with Bree.

"I'm so sorry!" Nancy said. "I didn't mean to say that."

"Yes you did! Some best friend you are!" Bree's voice sounded wobbly.

"I didn't mean to hurt your feelings!" Nancy's voice got wobbly too. "I feel awful! I don't know why I said that stuff!"

"Leave me alone!"

Nancy could tell that Bree meant it.

Bree ignored Nancy for the rest of the day. When school was over, she hurried ahead of Nancy to the bike rack and rode home by herself.

CHAPTER 9

# DRESS REHEARSAL

That night Bree didn't answer any of the messages of apology that Nancy sent in their Top-Secret Special Delivery mail basket. She refused to come to the phone when Nancy called.

The next day in school, Bree was still giving Nancy the silent treatment. When the third-grade girls were changing backstage for the dress rehearsal, Nancy saw Bree in her costume for the first time.

"You look so chic!" Nancy told her. In French that meant stylish.

Bree had on a short flouncy skirt, a T-shirt that said *I ♥ NY* and a green foam rubber crown with points, a souvenir from when Bree's family had visited the Statue of Liberty.

Without even glancing at Nancy, Bree tapped off. *Clickety-click-click.*

Bree did not have a forgiving nature. When she got mad, she stayed mad. But by now Nancy had hoped they'd be friends again. With a heavy heart, Nancy pulled on her cowboy boots, grabbed her guitar, and walked out onstage.

"Hey! No fair!" Grace said the second she laid eyes on Nancy. "You copied me!" She was trying to shout, only her voice cracked.

Nancy did a double-take. She and Grace looked almost like mirror images of each other. Even their cowboy boots were the same color pink.

"Mr. D, tell her to change!" Grace said. "I'm the star of the Oklahoma number. I have to look—" Grace stopped to sneeze. "I have to look special."

Mr. Dudeny said, "Grace, it's perfectly fine if you both are dressed like cowgirls." Then he clapped his hands for silence. "Ready, everyone! Emcee, where are you?"

Today was Lionel's first day back in school. His costume looked great. He was dressed up like Uncle Sam in a top hat, blue jacket, and red-and-white-striped pants. But he had to keep blowing his nose between jokes. And his voice sounded hoarse. There was something wrong with Grace's voice too. Before she started the Oklahoma song, she blasted her throat with a can of throat spray.

"Oklahoma! Where the wind comes sweepin' down the plain!" Grace's voice kept cracking. It sounded like a chicken squawking.

"I want to start over," Grace croaked to the teachers. She ran for the throat spray. But after the opening line, Mr. Dudeny made her stop. "Grace, trying to sing is hurting your throat. My advice is to give it a rest for now."

"But I'm not sick! Honest!" Grace said. She was blinking really hard. And her mouth was clamped shut in a tight line. Nancy was stunned. Grace looked as if she was about to cry.

Mr. Dudeny went over to Grace and said something that Nancy couldn't hear but that made Grace stomp off the stage. "It's not fair. I feel abso—" Grace started coughing before she could finish the sentence.

The dress rehearsal was the last time on Thursday anyone in 3D saw Grace.

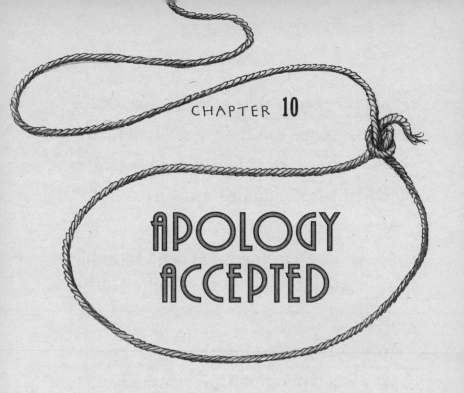

# CHAPTER 10

# APOLOGY ACCEPTED

"Grace had to go home early," Olivia told Nancy on the phone that evening. "She's sick. She's going to miss *The Nifty Fifty*! Mr. D called each of us in the Oklahoma number. We all know the song, so we're going to do it without her."

"Poor Grace," Nancy said. She couldn't

remember ever feeling sorry for Grace before. But she did now. Really and truly sorry. Grace's big moment in *The Nifty Fifty* had been snatched away from her!

After saying good-bye to Olivia, Nancy called Grace. "I'm sorry you can't be in the show," she told her. "I feel really bad for you."

"You do?" Grace rasped.

"Yes. It's not fair you got sick."

"It sure isn't. Well—lookit. I hope you and Robert do okay." Then Grace told Nancy her throat hurt too much to talk anymore.

After hanging up, Nancy plopped onto her bed and stared over at Bree's window. The light was on in her room, but there was no sign of her. Was Bree nervous?

Was she excited? Was Bree wondering if Nancy was nervous and excited?

Nancy's father poked his head in her room. "Feeling a little jittery?" he asked.

Nancy shrugged. "I guess."

Her dad sat down beside her on the bed. "You know the old trick for staying calm, don't you?"

"No. What?"

"Right before you start, you look out at the audience and pretend that everyone is in their underwear!"

Nancy wrinkled her nose. "Eww. Daddy, I don't want to picture the parents undressed!" Then all of a sudden Nancy turned to her dad and blurted out what was really bothering her. "Bree and I are in a fight. I—I said stuff behind her back.

It was mean."

Her father looked surprised. "Why? Were you angry for a reason?"

"No, Daddy. I have no excuse. I made fun of how much she's practicing. Now I don't even care about *The Nifty Fifty*. Being in the show won't be any fun if Bree and me aren't speaking."

Her father was nodding. "You need to make things right."

"I've tried, Dad! Honest! She won't accept my apology."

"Try one more time."

"It won't do any good," Nancy insisted.

"Maybe not. But if you don't give it a shot, you definitely won't get anywhere."

"Hmm. I see your point." Nancy hauled herself off the bed. "I guess I could go over to her house and wait at the front door. I'll say I'm not leaving until Bree forgives me. I'll say I'm prepared to stand outside all night if I have to."

"Sounds like a plan. Hope you're back before dawn!"

Before she could change her mind, Nancy took the stairs two at a time and burst out the back door. She almost ran smack into Bree.

They both jumped back a step and looked at each other, startled.

"Where are you going?" Bree said.

"Over to your house. To beg your forgiveness." Then Nancy looked puzzled. "Why are you here?"

The expression on Bree's face was hard to read. It was halfway between a frown and a smile. Then she threw up her arms and said, "Because I can't stand being in a fight anymore! I want to be friends again. Apology accepted!"

"You mean it?" Nancy's hand flew to her mouth. "Oh, thank you! Thank you from the bottom of my heart!"

Nancy and Bree fell on each other, hugging.

"It wasn't nice what you said," Bree said

a moment later. "But my mom says you had a point. She thinks I go overboard and push myself too hard. I have tap-danced so much, I'm starting to get blisters on my blisters!"

"You'll be stupendous tomorrow."

"I hope. And then I never have to listen to that song about New York again," Bree said with a giggle. "Not for as long as I live."

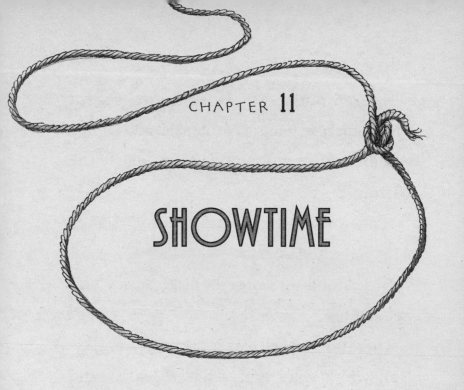

# CHAPTER 11

# SHOWTIME

I t was almost showtime! The scenery—a giant map of the US in red, silver, and blue glitter—was stapled across the back wall of the stage. Everyone was in costume. To Nancy, the kids no longer looked like ordinary third graders. They were now the cast members of *The Nifty Fifty*.

Even though Mr. D said peeking at the audience wasn't professional, Nancy couldn't resist pulling back the edge of the curtain.

"I see your parents and Freddy," Nancy whispered to Bree.

Bree stood on tiptoe behind Nancy and peeked too.

The auditorium was still pretty empty. Nancy's family had arrived early and grabbed front-row seats. Her dad was fiddling with his video cam. Her mom's back was turned because she was talking to another mom in the second row. JoJo was shouting to Bree's brother and pointing to an empty seat beside her. Nancy was not surprised to see that JoJo had worn her Cowgirl Sal hat and badge.

Bree straightened her crown for the fiftieth time. "I wish I didn't go on so soon."

"You're lucky!" Nancy said. "You'll be all done and you can relax. Robert and I don't go on till the end."

At that moment Mr. D came and shooed them offstage. Then the curtains parted and Lionel, dressed as Uncle Sam, roller-skated onstage.

"Greetings, my fellow Americans," Lionel began. "Welcome to *The Nifty Fifty*. Do we have a show for you! Our opening act is about the fiftieth state. That's Hawaii, for any parents in the audience who failed social studies. . . . And speaking of Hawaii, that reminds me of a little joke. A very little joke . . . What did one volcano say to the other?" Lionel took off his top hat and waited half a second. "I lava you!" he shouted. Then he pulled a rubber chicken out of his hat, bonked himself on the head with it, and roller-skated offstage.

*The Nifty Fifty* had begun.

For "Blue Hawaii," a line of girls in grass skirts danced the hula while a boy from the other third grade class lip-synched along with Elvis Presley. He wore a loud print shirt and his hair was slicked back in a poufy style called a pompadour.

After "Blue Hawaii," a bunch of kids in parkas and ski hats sang "North to Alaska." Then five couples did a dance from the olden days, called a waltz, to a song about Tennessee. After Lionel told a couple of more jokes and bonked himself with the rubber chicken, suddenly it was Bree's turn.

When the curtains opened, Bree was posed like the Statue of Liberty, her torch—a flashlight with orange crepe-paper flames—raised high.

"East Side, West Side," the music began.

Watching Bree, Nancy had to admit it: being a perfectionist paid off. Bree didn't miss a step. In fact, she made tap dancing look easy. *Clickety-clack-clack.* Her feet looked they were flying.

At the very end of the song, Bree tossed her torch—Mr. D was standing by, ready to catch it—and then did three almost-perfect cartwheels off the stage.

Nancy clapped till her hands stung.

"I did it!" Bree said. Her shoulders were heaving up and down, she was breathing so hard. Nancy couldn't remember ever seeing Bree look happier.

After Bree's dance, it seemed to Nancy as if time speeded up. The production numbers began and ended, one after another, almost in a blur. For the song

"California Girls," kids wore bathing suits and pretended to surf on boogie boards. Olivia and the Oklahoma chorus sang while they square-danced, followed by a song about the Rocky Mountains in Colorado that Nancy didn't remember hearing before.

Then Lionel was back onstage, telling a joke about Texas.

Nancy grabbed her guitar. She and Robert were next. Strangely she didn't feel at all nervous.

"If a cowboy rides into Houston on Friday and leaves a day later on Friday, how on earth can that be?" Lionel scratched his head, looking puzzled, then yelled, "Because his horse is named Friday!"

The curtains closed. Quickly Nancy

made a fake campfire out of branches from her backyard while Robert set out a couple of cardboard cactus plants.

Nancy sat down with her guitar by the fire and tilted her cowboy hat a little. Robert gave her a thumbs-up and disappeared offstage with his lasso. Then the curtains opened again.

*Sacre bleu!* The place was packed! Lots of people didn't have seats and were standing in the back. Everybody was looking at her. Every single person in the auditorium. So Nancy smiled. Or at least she tried to. Her lips didn't seem to be working properly. And then . . .

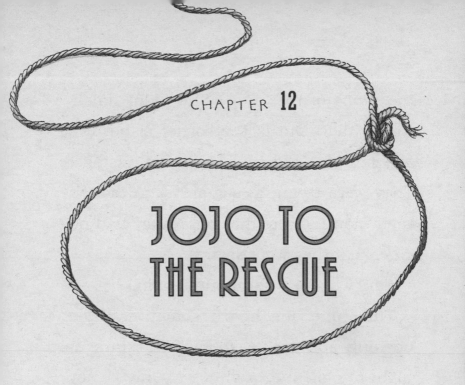

# CHAPTER 12

# JOJO TO THE RESCUE

Zap! Her mind went blank. Totally blank. It was the strangest feeling ever—like a giant eraser was inside her brain, wiping out everything.

Nancy opened her mouth. Nothing came out. What were the words to the song? She couldn't remember! What was the *name* of the song? She didn't know that, either! Out of the corner of her eye she saw Mr. Dudeny and Robert offstage. They were trying to signal her. Although their mouths were moving, Nancy had no clue what they were saying.

Nancy opened her mouth again.

This time she heard something—the opening line of the song. "The stars at night are big and bright . . ." Only Nancy wasn't the person who was singing.

It was JoJo.

JoJo had scrambled out of her seat in the front row. In a nanosecond she was onstage, sitting next to Nancy by the fake campfire.

Like magic, all the words to the song flew back in Nancy's head. She sang and played "Deep in the Heart of Texas" straight through with no mistakes, just as she'd rehearsed it so many times. Robert even added a new lasso trick, making the rope spin low to the ground at his side.

Every time they came to the chorus line, JoJo clapped four times. Soon everybody in the audience was clapping along too.

At the end of "Deep in the Heart of Texas," they all took a bow. Nancy, Robert, and JoJo. A trio. Not a duet.

There was lots of applause. Nancy's mom jumped up clapping. So did her dad, who let out piercing whistles through his fingers. JoJo hugged Nancy, then ran back to her seat right before the curtains closed. Backstage, Bree came rushing up to Nancy. "Are you all right, *chérie*?"

"I don't know what came over me!" Nancy covered her eyes. "I took one look at the crowd and . . . and just froze."

"Lookit," Robert said, "you only messed up for a second. After that it went okay."

There was no more time to talk because Lionel was in front of the curtains, announcing the grand finale. "Folks, it's the moment you've all been waiting for, when this show *finally* ends!"

Nancy found her *Hooray for the USA!* sign and was standing in place onstage when the curtains parted. The music to "This Land Is Your Land" started playing. It was her favorite song in the show, but right now it didn't cheer Nancy up. Hiding behind her sign, she marched around with all the other third graders. Soon the parents joined in too, so by the last line of the song—"Yes, this land was made for you and me"—the whole auditorium was filled with sound.

Then the curtain came down one final time.

*The Nifty Fifty* was over.

CHAPTER **13**

# ALMOST FAMOUS

**N**ancy skipped the cast party in the cafeteria. She wanted to go straight home. However, her parents insisted on going out to Cohen's Ice Cream Shoppe. "To celebrate," they said. Nancy barely touched the chocolate caramel parfait that she ordered.

"You got stage fright," her mom said. "It can happen to anybody."

"But I wasn't even nervous beforehand," Nancy said, spooning up a little whipped cream. "I knew the song inside and out!"

"That's how it happens. Stage fright just comes out of nowhere," her dad said.

"I was a good helper," JoJo said, her face smeared with chocolate sauce.

"You sure were!" her mom said. "You were a great helper." She turned to Nancy. "You know, Bree's parents thought JoJo was part of the act. They thought you froze on purpose."

"Oh, come on, Mom." Nancy took a tiny bite of ice cream.

"That's what they said. Both of them. JoJo was in a cowgirl costume, after all."

"Cowgirl *Sal*," JoJo corrected.

"Nancy, you were brave and stuck it out. And the song turned out great," her dad insisted. "I've got it all on the video cam!"

Video cam. *Sacre bleu!* Nancy put down her spoon and looked at her father. "Dad, just promise me one thing. Whatever you filmed, destroy it!"

That night all through dinner the phone never stopped ringing. Finally Nancy's mom answered it in case something bad had happened.

From the conversation, Nancy could tell the call was from her uncle Cal in Colorado.

"Wait, wait. Slow down!" her mom was saying. "It's on what? Are you kidding? No, no, we haven't seen it!"

Ooh la la! This didn't sound like bad news. It sounded like something thrilling.

"Let me talk to Uncle Cal." JoJo tried snatching the phone. But Mom shooed her away. "Okay, Cal. I'll look right now. Talk to Doug." Nancy's mom handed over the receiver. Then she ran and got her laptop from the den, pushed away her plate, and started typing furiously.

"What's going on?" Nancy asked.

Her mom didn't answer; her fingers kept hitting computer keys.

"Cal, how many hits?" her dad was saying. A second later he blew through his lips. "Whoa! That's unbelievable. Yup. Claire's searching right now."

"I think I found it!" her mom shouted. "Yes. I found it!"

Her dad hung up and raced to the laptop.

"Found what?" Nancy demanded to know. "Will one of you please tell me what's going on?"

"You're on YouTube!" her dad cried.

"SAY WHAT?!" Nancy yelped.

"Somebody at *The Nifty Fifty* put up a clip of your song. You and JoJo and Robert."

"Me? I want to see!" JoJo scooted onto Mom's lap.

"It's getting hundreds of thousands of hits," her dad went on. "It's going viral!" Then he started doing an absurd victory dance around the table.

"You mean all over America people are watching me make a fool of myself?" Nancy clutched her head. "This is the worst news ever!"

"No, Nancy! No, it's not." Her mom was replaying the video. "Everybody under-stands about stage fright. But you kept on singing and—aw, look, Doug!—it's so great when JoJo joins in!" Nancy's mom planted a kiss on JoJo's forehead.

"Daddy, did you have something to do with this?" Nancy said.

Her father stopped dancing. "Absolutely not! Scout's honor."

"I want to watch again," JoJo said.

"Well, I never want to see it!" Nancy bolted from the kitchen. Then, midway on the stairs, she stopped in her tracks. "No! I have to."

Nancy came back to the kitchen and forced herself to watch as her mother hit the replay arrow. What Nancy saw was horrifying.

There she was in the vest and red cow-boy hat, holding her guitar. At first there was a smile on her face. Then the smile vanished and her mouth started opening and closing like a goldfish. And her eyes looked weird. They were just staring into space, like she was hypnotized or under a witch's spell.

A moment later, the camera swiveled from Nancy onstage to the front of the auditorium. Although you could hear JoJo singing, at first all you saw was the backs of people's heads in their seats. Then there was JoJo, climbing up the steps to the stage and sitting beside Nancy.

Everything went fine after that. But the beginning of the act! The fish face! It made Nancy shudder.

Just then the doorbell rang. It was Bree. She came racing in. "*Chérie!* I just saw it!"

"You know already!"

"Grace called me."

"She's seen it too?" Nancy yelped.

"Everybody has!"

"What! Oh, I could die! I could just shrivel up and die," Nancy wailed.

"No! Don't be upset. Grace is jealous. She's scared you're going to get famous."

"As if that will ever happen!"

"Do you know that some girl our age was on the *Today* show all because of a song she sang on YouTube?"

Nancy nodded. "Yeah, my dad told me about her."

Bree spread her arms as if to prove her point. "Face it, Nancy, it could happen. You could be on national TV."

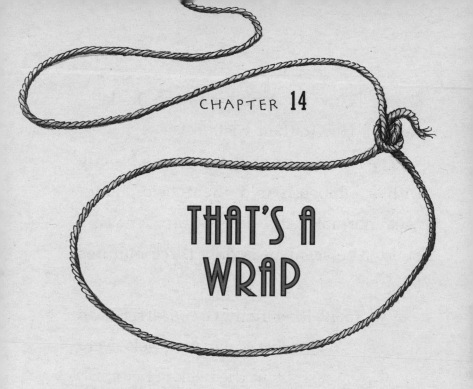

CHAPTER **14**

# THAT'S A WRAP

Nancy never appeared on national television. However, the local station WJIM did request an interview on Sunday morning. The show was called *Weekend Wrap-Up with Kelly Green.*

Nancy, Robert, and JoJo sat under hot lights in the studio in white plastic swivel chairs. Tiny microphones—ooh la la!—were clipped to their vests.

"Try not to look at the cameras," a guy with a clipboard told them beforehand. "Act normal. And keep your answers short. The segment is only three minutes long."

A moment later Kelly Green arrived on the set. A bunch of paper towels were stuck in the neck of her shirt. "It's to keep makeup off my clothes," she explained, shaking hands.

Once the paper towels were removed, her hair combed and sprayed, she took her place in a swivel chair between Nancy and Robert.

"Okay. We're good to go," someone behind the cameras shouted.

"Welcome to *Weekend Wrap-Up*. This is your host, Kelly Green, and I am happy to have three special guests here with me this morning—Nancy Clancy, her sister, Josephine Clancy, and Robert Nelson, who is one of Nancy's third-grade class-mates at the Ada M. Droozle Elementary School."

Kelly Green crossed her legs and clasped her hands together. "Last Friday what started out as one song in a patri-otic school variety show called *The Nifty Fifty* quickly went viral on YouTube. As of this morning the clip of these youngsters performing 'Deep in the Heart of Texas' has been watched by more than four million people." Kelly Green winked at Nancy, Robert, and JoJo. "That's pretty amazing, guys. So let's see what all the excitement is about."

After the clip was shown, Kelly Green asked, "How does it feel to be a YouTube sensation? Robert, why don't we start with you."

Unfortunately, Robert's microphone malfunctioned. That meant it wasn't working, and JoJo, who normally loved attention, totally clammed up. So that left Nancy to do all the talking.

The guy with the clipboard held up a sign that said *Only 20 seconds*. So Nancy spoke quickly. She tried to sound natural and mature. "At first I was despondent about getting stage fright. It was a mortifying experience. However, I am grateful to my sibling for her assistance." Nancy turned to JoJo, who was busy spinning in the swivel chair. "Actually, I am astonished that JoJo's being so bashful and timid. Ordinarily she is very rambunctious. In fact—"

"Gee, I'm afraid that's all the time we have," Kelly Green broke in. "Thank you so much, Nancy, Robert, and Josephine, for appearing on *Weekend Wrap-Up*, and now a word from Otto's Chevrolet, because if you need an auto, you oughtta go to Otto's!"

"That guy said the segment was going to be three minutes," Robert told Nancy as they all left the studio. His stopwatch was cupped in his hand. "But I timed it. It was only two minutes and fifty-four seconds."

Waving good-bye to Robert and his parents, Nancy climbed into the backseat of the car with JoJo.

Nancy's mom had taped the show beforehand so they could all watch as soon as they got home. She turned to the backseat. "Nancy, it was really sweet of you to give JoJo a shout-out on TV."

As soon as her mother said that, Nancy realized something. Yes, she had thanked her sister on TV, but she had never said anything just to JoJo. Face-to-face.

Nancy helped JoJo with the belt of her car seat. "JoJo, *merci mille fois*—that's French for 'Thank you a thousand times.' You're a great sister and you really came to the rescue."

"Is my posse buckled up?" Dad asked.

"Okay—back to the ranch!"

He started the car.

"The stars at night are big and bright," Dad began singing.

All the Clancys joined in. *Clap. Clap. Clap. Clap.*

"Deep in the heart of Texas."

# DON'T MISS

BOOK 6

NANCY CLANCY

Soccer Mania

WRITTEN BY
Jane O' Connor

ILLUSTRATIONS BY
Robin Preiss Glasser

# NANCY CLANCY,
## Soccer Mania

Read on for a sneak peek!

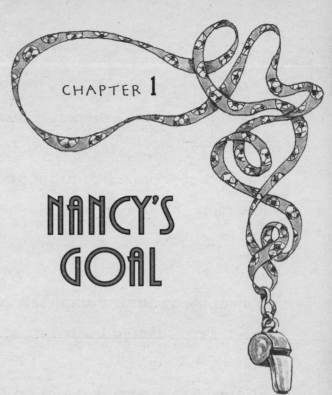

# CHAPTER 1

# NANCY'S GOAL

Soccer practice had just ended.

"All I want is to be mediocre," Nancy told Bree. Mediocre meant being average, or in the middle. "That's not asking much. I'll never be great. But I hate being terrible." Nancy sighed. "Mediocre. That's my goal."

"You *are* mediocre," Bree assured her. Then she said in a whisper, "Clara is way worse than you. So is Yoko. So is Tamar. Well—" Bree stopped to think about that some more. "Actually, you and Tamar are tied." That was one of the superb things about Bree. Nancy could always count on her best friend to be completely honest.

"No, Bree," Grace butted in. "Nancy is worse than Tamar."

Nancy could always count on Grace to listen in on private conversations. It was like her ears had superpowers!

"Nancy, face it. You can't dribble. You don't have any control of the ball. And you get so scared whenever somebody kicks it to you. You're like—" Grace put her hands in front of her face and trembled as if she

were watching a horror movie.
"And you're scared of
falling. Look how clean
you are!"

Grace's T-shirt
and shorts were
covered in grass stains.
Nancy's were spotless.

Grace was right. But the
way she pointed out stuff wasn't
the same as how Bree did.

"You and I are tied for best
on the team," Grace said to
Bree. Their team was called the
Green Goblins. "Then come Rhonda
and Wanda. But neither of them can intercept like you."

Intercept meant getting the ball away

from a player on the other team. It was amazing, astounding, almost superhuman how speedy Bree was. Nancy's dad, who was their coach, called her Bolt. That was short for Lightning Bolt, because Bree could dribble fast with the ball and zigzag in between other players.

"I can't wait for our first game," Grace went on. It was on Saturday, only three days away. "Bree, you and I are going to rule!" Then they all reached into a bowl of oranges that were cut into quarters. Refreshments were Nancy's favorite part

of soccer. When Bree and Nancy finished sucking out the juice, they smiled widely. The orange peels were still stuffed in their mouths.

"Hold it!" Nancy's dad said. He whipped out his smartphone for a photo.

Orange-peel smiles looked so absurd.

In the car on the way home, Nancy's dad said, "We're really coming together as a team. Bolt, love that fancy footwork! And Nancy, you are staying much more focused. During the scrimmage you always knew where the ball was."

"*Merci*," Bree and Nancy said at the same time.

Nancy's dad always had a compliment for her. She understood. He was trying to build up her confidence, but anybody, even the worst player in the world, could watch the ball. So Nancy said, "It's okay, Dad. I know I'm pretty bad." Then she told him the same thing she had told Bree before. "My goal is to become mediocre."

Bree and Nancy were in the backseat. Nancy could see her dad looking at her

through the car's rearview mirror. "No. No. Definitely wrong. Your goal is not to be mediocre. . . . Your goal is to score a goal." Then her dad cracked up at his own joke.

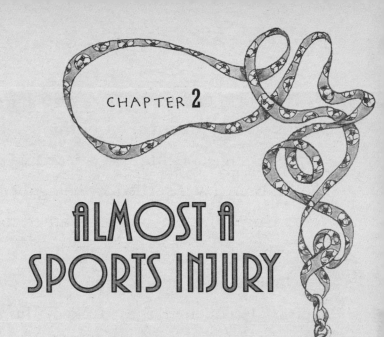

CHAPTER **2**

# ALMOST A
# SPORTS INJURY

"Come on. Let's do some more drills," Bree said as the car pulled into the Clancys' driveway. "We have time before it gets dark."

"Are you serious? I'm pooped." All Nancy wanted to do was collapse on the living room sofa. But Bree was out of the car and tugging Nancy by the arm.

9

"Practice makes perfect," Bree said. She said that about a lot of things—like tap-dancing, spelling, even learning pig Latin. Bree never settled for being mediocre at anything. She always wanted to be superb.

Nancy's dad heard Bree. "That's the spirit!" He opened the trunk of the car and tossed a soccer ball to Nancy.

"Okay, okay," Nancy muttered. Between her dad and Bree, it was two against one. She was outnumbered.

In the backyard, JoJo was pulling Freddy in her wagon. They were pretending to be on the way to a fire.

"Can you guys please play on the deck?" Bree asked. "Nancy and I need to practice soccer."

"No. We were here first," JoJo said.

"What if we let you play with us?" answered Bree.

"Big mistake!" Nancy told Bree at the same time JoJo and Freddy shouted, "Yes!" They ditched the wagon, took Frenchy into the house, and then listened to Bree explain some rules. Bree bent down on one knee with her hand on the ball, just the way Nancy's dad did while

talking to the team. It made Bree look very professional. "It's not like catch. You can't use your hands. All you can do is kick the ball."

"I don't like that rule," Freddy said.

"Too bad," Bree told her brother. "That's how soccer is played."

After they spread out, Bree said, "I'll kick to Nancy and she'll kick back to me. Then it's your turn, JoJo. Freddy, you go third." Bree let out a whistle and passed the ball to Nancy. But before Nancy had a chance to return it, JoJo ran in front of her and kicked the ball—really hard for a little kid. Nancy watched it whiz back to Bree.

"Nice one, JoJo." Bree looked as surprised as Nancy was.

# A CHAPTER BOOK SERIES
# ❀ STARRING EVERYONE'S ❀
# FAVORITE FANCY GIRL

## HARPER
*An Imprint of HarperCollinsPublishers*

www.fancynancyworld.com